Squishy McFluff
The Invisible Cat

Supermarket Sweep!

by *Pip Jones*

Illustrated by *Ella Okstad*

FABER & FABER

Squishy McFluff
The Invisible Cat

Supermarket Sweep!

For Ava, Ruby and Dan, my fabulous family,
I love you all THIS MUCH! xxx

First published in the UK in 2014
First published in the USA in 2017
by Faber and Faber Limited
Bloomsbury House
74–77 Great Russell Street
London WC1B 3DA

Designed by Faber and Faber
Printed in Malta

978–0571–30252–9

FSC
www.fsc.org
MIX
Paper from
responsible sources
FSC® C022612

4 6 8 10 9 7 5 3

Can you see him? My kitten?

He has eyes big and round.

His miaow is so sweet

(but it makes not a sound).

Imagine him quick!

Have you imagined enough?

Oh, good! You can see him!

It's Squishy McFluff!

One sunny morning,

in a house on a hill,

When the sky was quite blue,

the air warm and still,

A young girl called Ava

very happily sat

With Squishy McFluff,

her invisible cat.

They were planning a wonderful

day full of laughter,

Playing tricks in the morning,

climbing trees after.

Then launching a rocket!

And building a den!

Then football! And hopscotch!

And paddling! And THEN . . .

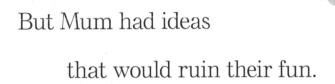

But Mum had ideas

    that would ruin their fun.

'Chop chop!' she yelled,

    'There are things to be done!

'We've shopping to do,

    we need food for the week.'

'Mum, that'll take AGES!'

    Ava's outlook was bleak.

McFluff had a brainwave . . .

so Ava said: 'Mummy!

'Squish has a TERRIBLE

pain in his tummy.

'A sore throat. A fever!

And PIMPLES! So surely

'He mustn't go out,

not when he's so poorly?'

11

Now Mummy, who secretly

found this delightful,

Knowing that shopping with

Squish would be frightful,

What with his habit

of causing such trouble,

Said: 'Put him to bed, Ava!

QUICK, on the double!

'Poor Squishy, how strange!

So sick, with no warning.

'He ate SIX invisible fish

just this morning.

'Yes, he should stay here,

and get himself strong.

'But you, Ava darling,

ARE coming along.'

Boo-hiss! The plan failed!

But Mum should have known

That Ava would not leave

her cat all alone –

She got in the back seat

as Mum turned the key,

With Squish on her shoulder

(of course, Mum didn't see) . . .

15

Well, wondering if things

could get any worse,

Ava sighed when Mummy said:

'Oh! Where's my purse?'

As Mum turned off the engine,

and quickly ran in,

McFluff looked at Ava

and then (with a grin) . . .

He jumped to the front seat!

So Ava did too,

To see what the shiny,

black buttons might do.

They twizzled and banged

ALL the knobs and the switches.

The wipers (on full speed)

had them in stitches.

But then, something happened.

The car went BERSERK!

And suddenly none

of the levers would work.

BEEP! BEEP! BEEP! BEEP!

The horn wouldn't stop.

The lights flashed and fizzed

'til the bulbs all went POP!

There were trumpets! And drum beats!

THE RADIO BLARED,

Disturbing the neighbours,

who shouted and glared.

Alarmed by the noise

and the neighbours' uproar,

Mum ran down the driveway

to open the door.

UP, DOWN! UP, DOWN!

CLICK! CLICK! CLICK! CLICK!

She tried and she tried,

but the locks were too quick!

And so getting herself

in a fuss and a panic,

Mum took out her mobile

and called a mechanic.

It took several hours

for the man to arrive . . .

So Ava and Squishy

enjoyed a long drive

To London! Then Scotland!

Then Spain! Then the Moon!

When he FINALLY came

    it was mid-afternoon.

He opened his toolbox

    and took out his pliers

To fix and replace

    all the hot frazzled wires.

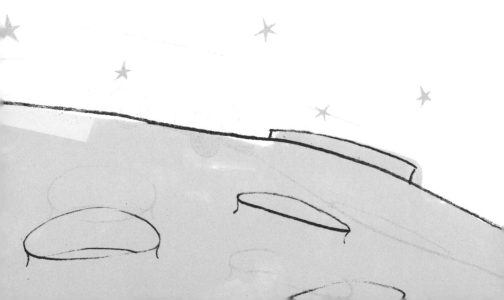

With everything mended,

    Mum said: 'I don't know

'What on **earth** happened here!

    Come on, let's go.

'We're off to that shop

    if it's the **last** thing we do . . .

'What a shame that poor Squishy

    couldn't come too.'

Ava and Squish were both

  good in the car.

(Well, the big supermarket

  was not very far.)

And Mum, as she drove there,

  happily chattered

About 'best behaviour'

  and how much it mattered.

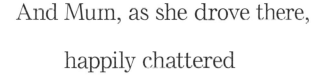

But oh, what a drag!

What a terrible bore,

When Ava and Squish

would MUCH rather explore

Outside in a forest,

among all the trees,

Getting mud on his paws,

and mud on her knees!

They'd be digging for treasures!

And searching for ELVES!

Not looking for pickles

and pastries on shelves . . .

By the time they arrived,

    McFluff had a plot

(He could always make fun

    where others might not).

The answer was staring them

    right in the face . . .

They grabbed a big trolley

    and started a race!

They hurried past veggies

and hurtled past fruit,

With Mum (and a man with a hat)

    in pursuit.

Feet like a blur,

    round a corner they dashed,

But they took it too quickly

    and, naturally . . .

CRASHED!

Oh bother . . . ! OH HELP!

All the parsnips and spuds

Tumbled around them

with crashes and thuds.

And the nimblest shoppers

leapt out of the way,

To avoid being splattered

by gooey fruit spray!

Mum caught them up,

    and gave Ava her 'look',

Which meant, 'There's ANOTHER

    black mark in your book!'

She wagged a long finger

    and said: 'That's enough!

'I assume you HAVE brought along

    Squishy McFluff?'

Ava grinned then replied,

with quite some bravado

For somebody **covered** in

squashed avocado:

'Well, actually YES!

And the funny thing was

'He perked up when I mentioned

an outing, because

'It's in a cat's nature,

exploring and prowling . . .'

Mum tapped her foot on the floor,

she was scowling.

'What if we help?' Ava smiled.

'We'll be good!'

Mum might not have nodded

if she'd understood . . .

Because just as soon as

she started the shopping,

McFluff and young Ava

both set about swapping!

42

Well, who in their right mind

would buy chewy greens

When the same price will buy

you a big bag of beans?

When Mum said: 'Ooh, pasta!

Yes that would be nice.'

McFluff knew that Ava

preferred chocolate mice.

And when Mum suggested

fresh fish for their tea,

McFluff pulled a face –

yuk! A fish he could SEE!

So Ava, not partial

to real fish herself,

Silently placed it

right back on a shelf.

'Dad won't miss prawns

or those smelly smoked kippers,

'Not when we show him

these huge **sherbet dippers**!

'Salad leaves? Cucumber?

Cheddar cheese? Ham?

'They can't be as scrumptious

as biscuits and jam!

'And at breakfast, instead of

those boring bran flakes,

'We'll put peanut butter

on top of these cakes.

'Ooh, good idea, Squishy!

A giant iced bun!

'I didn't know shopping

could be **this** much fun!'

And so they went on,

unaware of the shoppers

Who stared at their jellies

and giant gobstoppers.

Working so hard

to find things Mum had missed,

And the stuff she'd forgotten

to put on her list,

Fizz bombs and wine gums

and one chewy lolly

Were all very quietly

plopped in the trolley.

Too busy to notice

the things they were doing,

Mum hadn't a clue

of the naughtiness brewing

When she glanced at her daughter

and said with a smile:

'The last things on the list

should be in this aisle . . .'

Ava yawned

(it seemed

they'd been shopping for hours),

As Mum looked at air fresheners

made out of flowers,

Soap, floss and hand creams

scented with honey.

None of them seemed

the slightest bit funny.

But Squishy McFluff

had a brilliant idea!

So he (silently) miaowed it

for Ava to hear.

Then Ava said: 'Mummy!

Dad needs stuff for shaving!'

'Oh, does he? Thanks, Ava –

and thanks for behaving.'

But as soon as McFluff

got his paws on that foam

They sprayed Ava's head

'til she looked like a gnome!

They might have stopped there,

but oh, what a caper!

What fun to make clothes

out of pink tissue paper!

Boxes for shoes!

Toothbrushes in ears!

They were laughing so hard

they were almost in tears!

The rascals stopped giggling

when Mum said: 'Okay,

'I think we've got everything,

let's go and pay.'

The till lady shrieked!

'Oh my GOODNESS!' she said.

'What's wrong?' Mummy asked,

as her heart filled with dread.

Mum turned round slowly,

and went very white

When she clapped eyes on Ava . . .

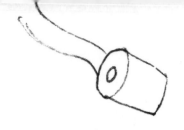

Oh crumbs, what a sight!

All wrapped in loo roll,

she looked rather weird

With her crazy square feet

and her bubbly beard.

Mum looked in the trolley

and noticed, at last

(With her hands on her hips

and completely aghast),

That rather than vegetables,

bread rolls and meats,

It was stuffed full of all sorts

of sweet, sickly treats.

'Where is the broccoli?

    Where are the PEARS?

'We CAN'T spend a week

    eating CAKES and ECLAIRS!

'Dad CAN'T make his omelettes

    with these CHOCOLATE eggs . . . !'

Squish slunk off and hid,

    right behind Ava's legs.

'THAT CAT!' Mum said crossly,

crinkling her brow.

'Tell him to get in my pocket

RIGHT NOW!'

'Ex-CUSE me please, madam!'

said the snooty cashier.

'I'm not one to butt in,

yet I MUST interfere.

'We CAN make exceptions,

and guide dogs are fine

'But I'm sorry, at cats,

well, we DO draw the line.'

Mum turned to the lady

and started explaining

But McFluff had seen something!

It looked entertaining.

Two looooong, dangly earrings!

He leapt up with a bounce

Then wiggled his bottom,

preparing . . . to . . . POUNCE!

'Madam! NO CATS. Now,

I'd be most obliged

'If you'd just find your kitten

AND TAKE HIM OUTSIDE!'

Mum sighed and said: 'Ava,

before we get banned

'Please point to McFluff

so she might understand?'

But, oh dear! Poor Mummy!

To her dismay,

Ava DID point,

then she started to say . . .

'Behind you, behind you!

Mind where you stand!

'He's right by your shoe!

Now he's sniffing your hand!

'He's climbed on your shoulder!

His tail's in your EAR!

'Look harder, turn quicker!

No, not THERE . . . he's here!'

The cashier went loopy!

'Your cat's a DISGRACE!

'Get him off, get him off!

He's invading my space!'

Swiping and shuddering

    and starting to shake,

The manager sent her

    for an early tea break.

Mum opened her pocket

    and stretched it out wide.

Then, frowning at Ava, said:

    'Put him INSIDE!'

McFluff clambered in,

his ears sadly flopping,

As Ava agreed she would do

proper shopping.

Fruit, fish and greens,

ingredients for cooking,

Were solemnly gathered

    while Mum **was** looking.

The groceries paid for,

    it seemed that was that –

But Mum didn't see

    Ava wink at her cat . . .

In the car, Ava

    whispered:

'Squish! Come to me!

'I've got something special,

just WAIT 'til you see!

'I'll have to eat stinky, real salmon

with Mummy

'But your tea will be perfect!

Scrumptiously YUMMY!

'Mum didn't see me,

it's a real **whopper,** Squish . . .

'I snuck in a great, big,

invisible fish!'

The End

About the author

Pip Jones lives in East London with her partner, her two daughters and a real invisible cat (it doesn't catch mice, but it doesn't need a litter tray either, so there are pros and cons). She writes a lot. She even owns a writing cloak! And she spends days on end working out how to get good rhymes, such as 'snuffle' and 'kerfuffle', into stories. Pip won the inaugural Greenhouse Funny Prize in 2012 with *Squishy McFluff: The Invisible Cat!*, her first book.

About the illustrator

Ella Okstad returned to her native Norway after graduating from the Kent Institute of Art and Design in 2000 where she now illustrates children's books for both Norwegian and UK publishers. Squishy is her first imaginary cat.